D0195827

SLEEPING B

A Story of Hope

Adapted by Lisa Harkrader
Illustrated by the Disney Storybook Artists

Published by Louis Weber, C.E.O., Publications International, Ltd.
7373 North Cicero Avenue, Lincolnwood, Illinois 60712

Ground Floor, 59 Gloucester Place, London W1U 8JJ

Customer Service: 1-800-595-8484 or customer_service@pilbooks.com

www.pilbooks.com

p i kids is a registered trademark of Publications International, Ltd.

Manufactured in China.

8 7 6 5 4 3 2 1

ISBN-13: 978-1-4127-6779-8

ISBN-10: 1-4127-6779-2

publications international, ltd.

Long ago in a faraway land, King Stefan and his queen celebrated the birth of their beautiful daughter, Princess Aurora.

Their friend King Hubert was also joyful about the royal birth because Aurora was betrothed to marry his son Prince Phillip one day.

Also celebrating the royal birth were three good fairies — Flora, Fauna, and Merryweather. Each fairy blessed Princess Aurora with a special gift.

"I give you the blessing of grace and beauty," said Flora.

"And my gift is the gift of song," added Fauna.

But before Merryweather could bless Princess Aurora with her special gift, thunder and lightning filled the castle, and the evil Maleficent appeared!

"The princess shall indeed grow in grace and beauty, but before the sun sets on her sixteenth birthday, she will prick her finger on the spindle of a spinning wheel and die!" declared Maleficent.

Then the evil fairy disappeared. Everyone gasped and looked to Merryweather to undo the evil curse.

"The only hope I can offer is that Princess Aurora will not die," said Merryweather. "She will sleep until she is awakened by true love's kiss."

Hoping to escape Maleficent's curse, the three fairies whisked Princess Aurora away to live with them in the forest. There, Aurora would be known as Briar Rose. The King and Queen were terribly sad, but they hoped that their daughter would return to them on her sixteenth birthday.

The years passed until Briar Rose's sixteenth birthday. While Flora, Fauna, and Merryweather prepared a birthday surprise for her, Briar Rose went for a walk in the forest.

Briar Rose loved spending time in the forest. She sang to the squirrels, birds, owls, and rabbits. She even shared her hopes and dreams with them. More than anything, Briar Rose hoped that she would fall in love.

As Briar Rose sang, her beautiful voice attracted the attention of a man passing by. It was love at first sight — just as she had always hoped!

Briar Rose rushed home to share the news that her true love had found her. He was going to come to the cottage that night to call on her.

The fairies broke the news gently to Briar Rose that she was really Princess Aurora and already betrothed to Prince Phillip.

"We are to take you home to the castle tonight," Flora explained.

"The King and Queen have been waiting sixteen years for your safe return," added Fauna.

The princess was heartbroken. She didn't want to marry Prince Phillip. With a heavy heart, she set out toward the castle with the fairies.

Meanwhile, Maleficent had been searching for the princess for sixteen years, but she had failed to discover her whereabouts until that very day. As the fairies and Aurora walked to the castle, they had no idea that Maleficent was waiting for them.

Upon arriving at the castle, Princess Aurora was hidden away until the moment of her return was to be announced. Suddenly, a mysterious light shone in her room. Under its spell, the princess walked toward the trap set by the evil Maleficent!

Aurora opened a door in the tower and saw a spinning wheel. She had never seen one before. After Maleficent had placed the curse on the princess, King Stefan had decreed that every spinning wheel in the kingdom be destroyed. He did not want to take any chances that Aurora would prick her finger and die.

As Aurora slowly approached the wheel, the evil voice of Maleficent whispered, "Touch the spindle. Don't be afraid. Touch it."

Aurora reached out to touch it and pricked her finger. The fairies soon discovered their beloved Princess Aurora lying on the floor.

When Prince Phillip called at the cottage that night, it was not Briar Rose he found, but Maleficent instead! She took him to the Forbidden Mountains and threw him in her dungeon.

"Your peasant girl is really a princess," said Maleficent. "She will sleep for a hundred years before awakening!"

At that moment, all hope was not lost. The good fairies arrived to help the prince escape.

"Take the Shield of Virtue!" said Flora.

"And the Sword of Truth!" said Fauna.

"You are our only hope!" cried Merryweather.

Prince Phillip fought bravely. He overcame Maleficent's evil curse!

In the castle, Prince Phillip found Princess Aurora sleeping. Kneeling beside her, he kissed her. Princess Aurora opened her eyes and gazed with gratitude at her true love. He was Prince Phillip! After that day, Princess Aurora and Prince Phillip lived happily ever after.

Sleeping Beauty: A Story of Hope

Hope means believing that something is possible.

It is the heartfelt excitement you feel when you wish for something to happen.

Everyone who loved Princess Aurora hoped she would be protected from the wicked Maleficent. They hoped that by taking her to live in the forest, she would be safe.

While in the forest, Briar Rose had hopes of her own. More than anything, she hoped to find her one true love. And that is exactly what happened.

Oftentimes, hope is the most important thing we have, because nothing can destroy hope — not even Maleficent's terrible curse!